A.F. HARROLD'S POCKET BOOK OF POCKET POEMS

BLOOMSBURY EDUCATION
Bloomsbury Publishing Plc
50 Bedford Square, London, WC1B 3DP, UK

Bloomsbury Publishing Ireland Limited, 29 Earlsfort Terrace
Dublin 2, DO2 AY28, Ireland

BLOOMSBURY, BLOOMSBURY EDUCATION and the Diana logo are
trademarks of Bloomsbury Publishing Plc

First published in Great Britain, 2025 by Bloomsbury Publishing Plc

This edition published in Great Britain, 2025 by
Bloomsbury Publishing Plc

Text copyright © A.F. Harrold, 2025

Illustrations copyright © Jack Viant, 2025

A.F. Harrold and Jack Viant have asserted their rights under the
Copyright, Designs and Patents Act, 1988, to be identified as Author
and Illustrator of this work

This is a work of fiction. Names and characters are the product of the
author's imagination and any resemblance to actual persons, living or
dead, is entirely coincidental.

All rights reserved. No part of this publication may be: i) reproduced
or transmitted in any form, electronic or mechanical, including
photocopying, recording or by means of any information storage
or retrieval system without prior permission in writing from the
publishers; or ii) used or reproduced in any way for the training,
development or operation of artificial intelligence (AI) technologies,
including generative AI technologies. The rights holders expressly
reserve this publication from the text and data mining exception as
per Article 4(3) of the Digital Single Market Directive (EU) 2019/790.

A catalogue record for this book is available from the British Library

ISBN: PB: 978-1-8019-9497-2; ePDF: 978-1-8019-9496-5;
ePub: 978-1-8019-9498-9

2 4 6 8 10 9 7 5 3 1

Printed and bound in the UK by CPI Group Ltd, CR0 4YY

MIX
Paper | Supporting
responsible forestry
FSC® C171272

To find out more about our authors and books visit
www.bloomsbury.com and sign up for our newsletters

For product safety related questions contact
productsafety@bloomsbury.com

A.F. HARROLD'S POCKET BOOK OF POCKET POEMS

BLOOMSBURY EDUCATION
LONDON OXFORD NEW YORK NEW DELHI SYDNEY

Introduction, part one
– Why I wrote this book ...

One of the things I enjoy is writing a poem onto a postcard, adding a name and address, sticking a stamp on it, and then dropping the postcard in the bright red pillar-box that's over the road.

Why do I like doing this? I like it because so much of the post we receive these days is either boring, or is just another pizza flyer.

It is a special thing to receive something handwritten, something that is unique to your doormat that morning, that was made for you.

My dad was a postman, and I was postman for a very brief time too, once, long, long ago, and I know that delivering the handwritten letters and postcards, the things that carried a little bit of human heart with them, was one of the things that made it such a good job.

And so I write poems on postcards, (a) because I know they will be a little bit special for the people receiving them to receive, and (b) because I know that the poems will also be read by the posties who carry them to your doors, and if I can cheer up cold mornings on their rounds with funny poems, then I feel I've done something good for the world.

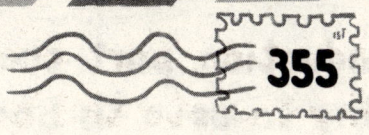

This means I have made myself a big store of short and very short poems that fit in that little bit of empty space on the left-hand side of a small rectangle of cardboard. And here they are.

(Another reason to like short poems is that they are short and are therefore either (a) easy to remember, if you like them, or (b) easily avoided if you don't. They don't overstay their welcome, unlike some poems, which go on and on and on and on for pages and pages and pages ...)

I encourage anyone and everyone to send poems or pictures on postcards, because this world could do with more art flying around it, unexpectedly, in all directions, for no reason at all.

AFH, 2025, just after breakfast

Introduction, part two
- How to use this book ...

When I get a poetry book I like to open it up at a random page and just read a poem, not knowing what I'm going to be getting. Then I can flick to another page and find another random poem completely different to the first one, or maybe a bit similar, or, if I'm really bad at flicking, exactly the same poem. Some people, however like a bit more order in their poetry books.

I've arranged the poems so that they get smaller as the book goes on. That way if you want a really quick poem, dip in near the back ... or if you've got a bit more time, take the plunge right up near the front. (The longest poems are only 60 words long, so even then you'll have time to catch the bus afterwards without needing to run.)

The poems are about all sorts of things, and although a lot of them are funny, some are reflecting on nature or time or life, and some are just a bit odd. And they're all sort of mixed up together, like kittens in a washing machine, except not as wet or dangerous.

But, just in case you wanted to find a poem on a specific theme or topic, I've made you the following 'Thematic Contents Index List Thingie', with page numbers. If you want a poem about someone called 'Susan', just look in the 'Animals (people)' section, trail your finger along until you reach 'Susan' (just after 'Sisters' and before 'Teachers'), read the page number ('142'), go find the page and read the poem, and 'Hey presto' words alive, you've found a poem that mentions 'Susan' (which is the name of my cat (but the poem isn't about my cat, it's about a different Susan, because there's more than one Susan in this world, as you probably already knew, because you're smart and possibly called Susan yourself)).

Have fun reading, whether you random dip or purposely plunge ...

AFH, 2025, just before tea

Thematic Contents Index List Thingie

Animals (birds)
Albatrosses – 15; Birds in general – 3, 13, 17, 21, 28, 60, 82, 106; Canaries – 129; Chickens – 49, 57; Ducklings – 150; Flamingos – 48; Geese – 145; Herons – 66; Penguins – 9, 38; Pigeons – 111; Ramírez – 9; Robins – 27, 99, 143; Seagulls – 62, 69; Sparrows – 73; Vultures – 75; Wrens – 82.

Animals (not birds (except snakes))
Anchovies – 40; Ants – 43; Armadillos – 114; Badgers – 25; Barnacles – 44; Bats – 112; Bees – 29, 66, 113, 122, 128; Butterflies – 24, 59; Camels – 30, 150; Cats – 21, 23, 24, 52, 58, 82, 157; Centipede – 62; Cheetah – 145; Cows – 49, 113; Crabs – 75; Crocodile – 135; Dogs – 35, 45, 73, 77, 115; Dolphin – 54; Dragonflies – 123; Fish – 28, 114, 125; Fleas – 75, 157; Flies, various types – 59; Giraffes – 46, 69; Goats – 36, 108; Headlice – 58; Hedgehogs – 52, 73, 115, 141; Horses – 141; Ladybirds – 33; Lambs – 144; Limpets – 44; Monkeys – 7; Mooses – 108; Octopuses – 44; Pigs – 108; Plankton –

114; Rabbits – 65, 77, 135, 157; Rhinoceroses – 121; Sheep – 40; Sloths – 69; Slugs – 14, 129; Spiders – 93; Squirrels – 3, 11, 87, 89, 140; Stoats – 75; Tigers – 52, 87, 111, 127; Wasps – 69, 75, 151; Whales – 103, 114; Wolves – 40, 43, 90, 108, 140; Worms – 21, 50.

Animals (people)
Babies – 29, 75; Bank Managers – 3; Bill – 67; Boxers – 110; Bridget – 72; Brothers – 2, 70; Charles – 11; Charlie – 107; Clowns – 142; Dave – 16, 59; Dentists – 80; Ethel – 133; Frances – 134; Gaston – 142; Graham – 107; Grandparents – 12, 71, 119; Mrs Hosannah – 91; Jenny – 10; Librarians – 85; Martin – 66; Mary – 144; Mo Finklestein – 10; Monks – 152; Morris – 107; Mr Potts – 33; Mrs Potts – 33; Nancy – 125; Parents – 10, 25, 37, 61, 67, 124, 130; Peter – 107; Phyllis – 142; Pirates – 101, 126; Postal Workers – 47; Richard – 77; Simon – 21, 63; Sisters – 2; Surprises – 148; Susan – 142; Teachers – 18, 31, 40, 112; Vegetarians – 126; Wanda – 149; William Blake – 99; Witches – 125; Zedric – 80.

Animals (snakes)
Snakes – 1, 6, 69, 91, 97, 109, 138, 153.

Animals (things that are like people, but different)
Ghosts – 16, 47, 112; Medusa – 148; Mermaids – 133; Snowmen – 37, 56, 94; Trolls – 108; Unicorns – 104; Vampires – 112; Werewolves – 160.

Bodies and Body Parts
Beards – 107; Bones – 136; Bottoms – 7, 25; Brains – 2, 51; Feet – 87, 153; Internal Organs – 5; Knees – 31; Noses – 2, 12, 31; Rashes – 58; Scabs – 58; Skeletons – 112; Skin – 136; Teeth – 80, 120; Toes – 29, 31, 55.

Food
Apples – 24, 51, 158; Berries – 12; Biscuits – 118; Bread – 20, 141; Brussels sprouts – 144, 156; Burgers – 108; Butter – 85; Cake – 88, 153; Carrots – 37, 94, 101, 135, 157; Cheese – 107; Chips – 122; Chocolate – 97; Chowder – 125; Coconuts – 57, 87; Crisps – 14, 15; Custard – 132; Dog Food – 155; Doughnuts – 5, 80, 97, 105, 155; Eggs – 49, 53; Fish Fingers – 149; Grapes – 128;

Gravy – 73, 107; Ham – 20; Honey – 29, 113; Humbugs – 92; Ice Cream – 56; Jam – 118; Kebab – 58; Kippers – 23; Lettuce – 135; Macaroni – 107; Marmite – 29; Mash – 58; Mayonnaise – 125; Milk – 49, 113; Pancakes – 88; Peanuts – 9; Picnics – 43, 53, 140; Pies – 63, 76; Potatoes – 144; Prawn Crackers – 20; Pumpkins – 47; Raisins – 65; Ratatouille – 58; Rolls – 120, 141; Sandwiches – 125; Sausages – 126, 139; Souffle – 20; Soup – 146; Spuds – 144; Sticky rice – 58; Strawberries – 34; Tea – 42; Toast – 25, 59; Toffees – 149; Yorkshire Pudding – 144.

Nature and Outdoors Things
Clouds – 15, 17, 24, 53, 100, 113; Cobwebs – 93; Flowers – 6, 24, 98, 143; the Moon – 13, 24, 43, 96; Mud – 124; Nettles – 75; Rainbows – 15; Rivers – 32, 72; Rocks – 120; the Sky – 17, 60, 77, 100, 106; Stars – 77; Stone – 95; Trees – 3, 11, 17, 21, 35, 60, 64, 81, 89, 93, 113, 154; Volcanos – 95.

Places You Might Go
Antarctica – 9; Airport – 8; Circus – 142; Countryside – 115; Desert – 150; Hospital – 128; Kitchen – 152; Mallorca – 40; School – 12, 14, 18, 43, 96; the Seaside – 8, 45, 56, 62.

Seasons and Weather
Autumn – 81, 93, 106, 154; February – 27; Fog – 100; Rain – 17, 32, 53, 62; Snow – 24, 27, 37, 39, 43; Spring – 98, 128, 143, 154; Summer – 38, 98; Thunder – 8; Winter – 8, 27, 60, 137, 143.

Special Days
Bathtime – 61, 62, 119; Birthdays – 22, 148, 155; Christmas – 144; Halloween – 132; Surprises – 148.

Stuff
Asthma – 4; Athletics – 4; Ballet – 88; Cannibalism – 56; Cuddling – 1, 23, 129; Dancing – 134; Drawing – 102; Dreams – 13, 16, 19, 115; Fruity Smells – 28; History – 18, 45; Juggling – 7; Laughter – 61; Mathematics – 109; Memory – 19, 130; Music – 130; Oblongs – 137; Pacifism – 110; Questions – 10; Reading – 19, 31; Royalty

– 45; Running – 4; Silence – 24, 79; Sport – 33, 85, 147; Squares – 137; Surprises – 148; Washing Up – 42.

Things (not vehicles)
Advent Calendar – 156; Beds – 50; Blue Things – 6; Books – 24, 51, 85, 115, 144; Boring Things – 84; Bricks – 22, 36, 131; Bubble Bath – 61, 119; Cars – 30; Clothes, misc. – 8; Colanders – 156; Curtains – 71; Eggs – 145; Fireworks – 61, 84; Footballs – 147; Furniture – 78, 150; Glasses – 71, 136; Gloves – 8, 115; Jokes – 61; Kettles – 75; Lamp-posts – 68; Lies – 729; Mirrors – 30, 86, 101, 148; Muck – 86; Mud – 124; Paper – 64, 85; Pianos – 91; Quilts – 70; Sand – 150; Sneezes – 31; Soap – 146; Socks – 8, 31; Spoons – 57, 132; Sticks – 77, 149; Trousers – 8, 25, 52; Umbrellas – 32; Watering Cans – 70; Wellies – 140; Words – 28, 41, 61, 74.

Vehicles
Aeroplanes – 26, 55; Bikes – 131; Buses – 26, 90; Helicopters – 15; Hot Air Balloons – 15; Trains – 13, 26, 111; Trousers – 8, 25, 52; Zeppelins – 15.

The Poems ...

DO NOT EAT!

FRAGILE

SNAIL MAIL

Snake Poem

The snake that offers hugs and cuddles
is just the start of several troubles.

The snake that says they'll hold you tight
is one whose hug's worse than their bite.

The snake that snuggles on the bus
is probably worth making a fuss
about.

I've nothing against a snake, you see,
so long as the snake's got nothing 'gainst me.

A Nose Poem

Her brother was a dedicated nose-picker.
Dedicated to the cause.

Each night she'd sharpen his nails
to claws,
but didn't say.

After six months
he'd whittled
his nose
away.

He's now working on his brain,
cos he'll remain
a dedicated picker all his days.

And she stays
a wicked sister
who doesn't know
when a joke's gone on
too long.

Trees Do Like Squirrels Too

The trees are cheerleading the birds.

Their arms are raised.

Their pom-poms are *pom-pom-pom*ming.

'Go, birds!' they shout.

'Birds, stay!' they say.

'Build your nests in me!'

'I'm your best tree!'

'I'll hold you up when your wings are tired!'

Bank managers and movie critics
would have you believe
wooden things
can't contain so much emotion.

But they are wrong.

The Asthmatic Racer

When I run I wheeze.

I run a bit more
then I lean on my knees
and wheeze.

When I tell them I'm just resting
they say that they're drug testing
and they take away the
canister from my inhaler

which leaves me
increasingly wheezy
which doesn't please me.

And if I run after that
I tend to fall flat.

Donor Card

In my wallet
you'll find my Donor Card,
in case my organs
are of use to someone
after my death.

You'll also find
my Doughnut Card,
in case my packed lunch
is uneaten.

I promise
they will be jamful,
not ring,
and dusted lightly
with snowy dreams of hard white sugar.

This isn't a reason
to run me down.

Blue Day

The forget-me-nots were blooming.
The bluebells rang round the forest.
Over the white cliffs improbable birds flew.

It was a blue day.
It was a new day.
It was a Tueday.

Inexplicably,
the 's' had gone missing in the night,
not to be found in the cold dawn light.

A snake went to speak and had a fright,
silently.

Juggles

Don't juggle in the jungle
if your juggling's not great.

Monkeys are judgemental
and they whisper mate to mate,

saying: 'Cop a lot of that chap
chucking juggles everywhere.'

And they turn away, embarrassed,
showing bottoms that are bare ...

which is, it must be said,
just the sort of thing

that distracts a trainee juggler
from their trainee juggling.

Are You Ready for the Weather?

At the airport
they have a windsock
to see where the wind is going.

At the beach
Dad wears a sunhat
to keep his bald head from glowing.

In December
I put on my raincoat
to keep me from getting wet.

But as far as I know
there aren't any thundergloves,
or snowshirts,
or unexpectedheatwavetrousers,
or peasoupfogpants …
yet.

The Penguin

Ramírez was a penguin.
A penguin with a peanut allergy.

Were Ramírez to eat a peanut
he'd swell up like a balloon

and pop.

Ramírez did not know
he had a peanut allergy

because he was a penguin
and lived in Antarctica.

All he had ever had to eat were fish.

Unfortunately, he was also allergic to fish.

Questions, Questions, Questions

Jenny asked her mother, 'Why?'.
Her mother said she didn't know,
but went and asked Mo Finklestein
in case he wished to have a go
at answering the question, 'Why?'
He didn't. And so to this day
Jenny hasn't got a clue.
What can you do? What can you do?
What, as they say, can you do?

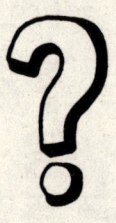

Can't See the Tree ...

Charles made a tree
out of bits of wood.

It looked pretty good.
It had leaves.
It had squirrels.
It was in the forest.

It was so good, in fact,
when he turned away
and turned back
he couldn't tell
which tree was his.

Which was quite annoying
since he'd put
so much effort into making it.

Very Berry

The fruits were so very tangy
on grandad's brambles
he called them blackverys.

Nothing beat
the steamed scent
coming out of his crumble.

So sweetly sticky
it stuck in your
nose hairs.

You took it to school with you
the next day,
and in boring lessons

you'd travel away
on the blackvery memory
of his blackvery crumble.

Dawn Choruses

It's dark outside
but the birds are singing.
The moon's still up
but the day's beginning.

The empty train
welcomes the driver –
that lunchbox-clutching
early arriver.

Back home someone's
noisily snoring,
dreaming the day
while it's still beforing.

It's dark outside
but the birds are singing.
The moon's still up
but the day's beginning.

Poem About Riding a Slug to School

Riding to school on the back of a slug
will make you (a) late
and (b) unpopular with the slug

(especially if you offer to share
your ready salted crisps,
as a reward,
when you finally get there).

So probably best
to not test out
this method of eco-friendly locomotion,
if that was your notion.

An Exercise in Taste

I've tried helicopter
and hot-air balloon,

and I've tried albatross
and Zeppelin,

and I've tried cloud
and rainbow,

but at the end of the day,
I have to say,

for the best taste of the sky,
so fast and vast and high,

cruising sedately
with an in-flight movie ...

it's plane crisps for me
every time.

Dave's Stories

Dave whispers
ghost stories
in your ear
when you're asleep.

He does it so quietly
you'll never wake up,
but will dream them.

It's like a magic gift he has,
this dream-whispering
ghost story
skill.

I have often slept
at his house
and the dreams have been ...
terrifying.

In conclusion,
Dave is very annoying.

Sky Poem

There's so much spare sky
some trees consider it a challenge
and live long lives
trying to fill it.

Others grow birds
on their long limbs
and send them off
to explore the wide blue space.

Either way
the sky never gets full
and clouds
still have room to lilo around,
leaking occasionally.

School

In my day school was very different.

For one thing,
there wasn't so much history to learn.
Lots of things that have happened now
hadn't happened back then.

For another thing,
the teachers were much younger.
Look at your teacher
and take twenty, thirty years off ...

why,
they were probably just kids themselves.

Remembery

I remember
  things that never happened.
I remember
  people I've never met.
I remember
  paths I've never gone down.
I remember
  promises no one made, or kept.

I remember
  silences I've snored through.
I remember
  views I've never seen.
I remember
  meals I've never eaten.
I remember
  the dark outside the dream.

Edible Arrangements

If you go to sleep in a hammock
made of ham hock,

or a bed
made of bread,

or on a sofa
made of soufflé,

or on a futon
made of prawn crackers,

then I wish you the best of luck
stuck,
as you are,
in a life weirder, even, than mine.

Birdlife

Impressed
by their singing
their feathers
and their flying
Simon climbed
his garden's tree
and built a nest
in the branches.

He gobbled worms
and sang joyously
at the sun's rising.

He flew arms out
with enthusiastic
amounts of flapping.

Nevertheless
featherless he fell
and, caught by the cat,
that was that.

To Be a Brick

To be a brick,
playing your part
holding up a house
where little kids live.

The things you'll see,
the things you'll share.

The laughter,
the tears,
the birthdays,
the fears,
the only getting to go on holiday
when the house falls down.

Oh! What a thing,
to be a brick.

This Poem is Not a Red Herring

I cuddled a kipper.
It was a cold kipper.
It was all alone.

The cuddled kipper's
no longer cold.
The cuddled kipper's happy.

It's been cuddled.
It's been warmed.
It's a cosy cuddled kipper.

Now my jumper smells of kipper.
I'm being followed by cats.
Perhaps they want to cuddle me.

Silences

Cat paws through the garden.
Butterflies in flight.
Morning daisies yawning.
The slowly falling night.

Snow before it's trodden.
Books before they're read.
The moon when freshly risen.
A secret left unsaid.

Clouds not ready to rain yet.
Fresh-stretching apple pips.
That moment between tick and tock.
Your finger-hushed lips.

My Special Mother

'Darling,'
my mother said,
'put your trousers on
before you eat your toast.'

This is the advice of hers,
I think,
that I appreciate the most.

She also sometimes said,
'Never look a badger in the bum.'

I wonder why?

What had the badgers done
to so upset
my mum?

Here, There, Everywhere

On the one hand,
buses know they're better
than trains.
Buses replace trains,
never the other way around.

On the other hand,
trains look down on buses,
waiting for engine trouble
and a level crossing
to teach them who's boss.

On the third hand,
planes look down on everyone.

February

Frost spins white lines
on the lawn,
grass turns glass-like,
crisp crackle-snap
underfoot.

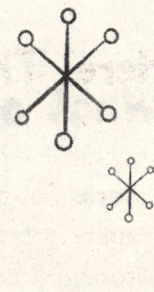

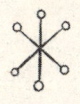

Robins puff themselves,
look as big as tennis balls,
as light as dandelions,
tap on the bird bath's
ice rink concrete.

There's the doorbell.
A blue-lipped lady
wants to come in.
The doormat
flutters with snow.

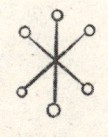

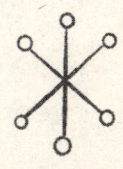

What are Poems Made Of?

I made you this poem.
I made it from words.

I could've been braver
and tried to use birds

or silver-bright fish
or an odd fruity smell,

but I don't think it would've
come out quite as well.

P.S. That smell isn't me, it's you.
(Check your shoe.)

Poem for a Baby with Seven Toes

This little bee went to market.
This little bee stayed at home.

This little bee had some nectar.
This little bee's on the phone.

This little bee made some honey.
This little bee's had a fright.

And this little bee's got confused
and seems to have made Marmite.

A Camel Carpet

A camel
makes a dreadful
carpet,

partly because of the lump (or lumps),

but mostly because,
as a pet for the car,
it takes up the whole back seat,

blocks the rear view mirror,

and has a tendency to spit
when startled,

which is bad
when you've carpooled.

Noses Belong on Your Face

Be thankful you have toeses
down there instead of noses.

Tenfold two-foot sneezes
would send tremors through your kneeses.

Your socks would get dead manky
if they doubled as a hanky.

Teachers would get bored repeating,
'Children, stop sniffing your feet in

quiet reading time, thank you.'

Umbrella Poem

Look at the fella
with the umbrella.

To him the rain
isn't a pain.

The light shower
lacks the power

to get
his hair wet.

It feels good,
this bundle of wire and cloth and wood.

But it won't help
when he falls in the river.

Spots and Dots

Mrs Potts
paints the spots
on the backs
of ladybirds.

Mr Potts
puts the dots
on the 'i's
of all my words.

There are lots
and lots and lots
of ladybirds
needing spots.

I try to keep
my poems short
so Mr Potts
can lend support.

Strawberry Poem

If you counted
all the pebbles
and gravels
and grits
and bits of sand
in the world
you'd have a heck of a job ahead of you.

Fruitless and unending.

Count instead
this single
simple
strawberry.

Fruitful and ending.

One strawberry.
One strawberry.
No strawberry.

Good Dog

This dog
doesn't realise
it is a Small Dog.

It is hauling
a stick
the size of

a Very Large Stick
or
a Fairly Small Tree.

It is proud.
It is strong.
It is brave beyond its height.

It is stuck
between
the gate posts.

Pet Envy

I've got two pet bricks.
One's good at doing tricks.

It'll sit when you tell it to,
stay when you tell it to too.

That's the list of the tricks it can do.
The other one can't even do that.

Next door's got a cat.

Snow Today, Gone Tomorrow

Snow thaws and eaves drip.
Snowman lilts and sags and dips.
His carrot nose is nicked by crows,
his scarf's reclaimed by Mum.

Footprints fade in melting snow.
To slush that special landscape goes.
Sleds are shedded, school is dreaded –
grown-ups happy, kids are glum.

Summertime (and I'm Glad I'm not a Penguin)

If I was a penguin
I wouldn't like the summer.

There'd be no snow to hide in,
there'd be no ice to slide on,

and as it's getting hotter
there's not a lot a

penguin like me
can do

but fret,
and maybe, also, sweat.

Glasshouses

People in glasshouses
shouldn't throw stones

and
people in stonehouses
shouldn't throw glass

and
people in snowhouses
shouldn't throw fire

and
people in firehouses
should get out quick
because their house is on fire
and that's never good news.

(Maybe they should throw
some snow.)

Yet More Advice

Never trust an anchovy
that mutters in its sleep.

Never trust a wolf
that's dressed up like a sheep.

Never trust a sheep
that's dressed up like a llama.

And never trust a geography teacher
who tells you the capital of Mallorca *isn't* Palma.

I Love All Words, Even the Misfits

Words flow like water from my pen –
a special sort of water,
which I call ink,
black as night.

Sometimes they're fine words,
sailing proudly, poemwards,

but sometimes they stink.

Holed below the waterline.

I still salute them
as they sink
out of sight.

The Fastest Man in the World Does the Washing Up

I've finished.

What really? When?

While you were writing the title.

Oh, goodness. You are fast, aren't you?

Yes.

Well, thank you, that's very kind. I'll put the kettle on.
Would you like a cup of tea?

Just a quick one, thank you.

Ants at the Picnic

Ants at the picnic
walking on the food.
Didn't ask first –
very, very rude.

Wolves in the wilderness
howling at the moon.
I'm trying to sleep –
it's a racket, not a tune.

Icy white snow
falling all night.
No school tomorrow –
sounds alright.

A Shellfish Poem

Kevin,
a barnacle,
clung
to the underside
of the ship
like a limpet.

The limpets
took offence
at his impression
and just let go,
drifting into the deep
like hard-edged snow.

Down below
octopi
put on hard hats
and prepared
to eat well.

Fighting the Waves

Whereas Canute
sat mute
and ineffectual
as the water lapped all
round his feet,

the dog at the seaside
puts up more of a struggle,
as if each bite, bark or tug'll
teach the sea
a lesson,

or so the king's men reckon.

Giraffes Sitting Down

Giraffes sit down when they want to
    play cards,
but they don't do it often because
    sitting down is hard
when your legs are as long as the
    giraffe's are,
and when they see they've got hooves ...
    the game never gets far.

Halloween Poem

At Halloween the postmen
and postwomen
huddle in the yard
inflating their punctured tyres
with vigorously wheezing bicycle pumpkins.

Fruity-puff, fruity-puff, fruity-puff.

This is probably why
the post is so often late.

That
and the fact
of all the ghosts and stuff.

Pink Sniffles

Flamingoes sneeze
when a cold wind blows.

The old pink birds
with the long wet toes

can't hold a hanky
to blow their nose,

so the way it is
is the way it goes

for the poor old
chill-toed,
drip-nose,
pink-winged
flamingo-go-goes.

The New Farmer Learns

I wish I'd then known then
what I now know now –
that it's eggs from the chickens
and milk from the cow.

You see, my first day was rainy,
but worse than that –
I drank chicken juice
with a soft-boiled pat.

Early Bird, Late Worm

Wise worms
  get up late,
stay in bed
  til half past eight,
or half past ten
  if really clever,
by then the birds
  have read the weather
report and all gone back to bed –
  now, safely, Worm
can raise its head.

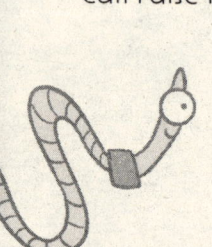

Why Books are Better than Apples

Eating books is easy.
You do it with your eyes.
Your brain fills up with stories –
a perfect priceless prize.

Unlike eating apples
this doesn't hurt the book.
It's still there on the shelf
so someone else can have a look.

Even Worser

There are worse things
than being eaten, slowly, by a tiger.

There are worse things
than finding your trousers are made
   of fire.

There are worse things
than accidentally swallowing a hedgehog.

There are worse things,
but probably not that many.

Ransom

I find a catnap in the morning
or a catnap in the afternoon
or a catnap in the evening or the night

is a lovely way to relax
and make a bit of cash,
but don't tell the RSPCA.

All right?

Just A Little Bit of Effort and Look What We Can Do

If clouds tried harder
they'd suck the rain
from the ground.

If lost things tried harder
they'd quickly be found.

If chickens tried harder
their eggs would be round.

If I tried harder
this poem would end
with a rhyming sound.

Pet-Picking Basics

Swimming lengths
at the pool
with your cat
is rather cruel.

Also cruel
is going golfing
with your
dolphin.

When buying a pet,
I suggest,
they should employ
a simple test:

the basic
requirement:
'Do you understand
this animal's preferred environment?'

Roots

It's a good picnic
to which you need carry no food,
simply slip off your shoes,
let your toes grow down,
rootling around,
deep into the soil,
supping and sifting,
as you palm up your hands
and drink
the sunshine.

At the Seaside

The snowman
on holiday
was sat upon the sand,

a hanky on his head
and
an ice cream in his hand.

He took another lick
and
a feeling in him grew:

I wonder if this was
somebody
that I knew?

If Coconuts were Eggs

In a world where the hens
lay huge furry brown eggs,

they've a tear in their eyes
and wide-apart legs.

Oh! Find me a spoon
that'll crack through the shell

and I'll dip my toast deep
in the shampoo-egg smell.

Manners Maketh

Don't scratch your rash
into Grandad's mash.

Don't flick your scab
into Mum's kebab.

Don't bury your headlice
in your dad's sticky rice.

Don't shave the cat
on your brother's ratatouille.

Just do unto others
as they'd do unto you-ee.

Why Dave Shouldn't Be Allowed to Name Things Anymore

The horsefly flew by with ...
    a clattering of hooves?

The dragonfly flew by with ...
    a crackling bonfire roar?

The butterfly flew by like ...
    the scrape of knife on toast?

The housefly flew by like ...
    the slamming of a door?

Winter Note

After rain
the sun comes out
and the
drip
 drip
  drip
of trees'
leaves
sparkles in my ears like simple melodies.

The sky turns blue
and the birds'
songs
trill as they hover
at the feeder
finding
glistening seeds.

Remembering Good

She had a way
to turn grey
to butterflies,

to turn a dull day
to fireworks –

sparking laughter
with dafter
and dafter
dancing words –

her jokes were plasters,
bubble-bath on winter nights,
forget-me-nots
and hold-me-tights –
she made things right.

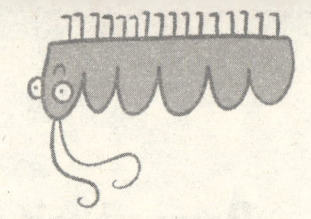

Centipede

You can't impede the scent of a centipede
anymore than a centipede can.

He's tried to wash more often,
in fact it's a personal goal,
but every time he turns on the tap
he's swept straight down the hole.

Seagulls are Smart

Seagulls in sou'westers
are standing by the shore.

They look like they're waiting
but they won't say what for.

I spend so long watching
I get drenched by the rain.

Then the reason for the waterproofs
becomes plain.

Piece of Pie

A chap called Simon
met a pie-man
going to the fair.

He bought a pie
for a reasonable price
and ate it. Right there.

Nothing funny happened.
Nothing weird occurred.

Or at least
that's the story I heard.

Poetry's Brutal Truth

Trees died
to make the paper
to make the pages
to make this book
to house these poems.

I keep my verses short
so the fewest trees need die

(but it's still a large number,
if they're bonsai).

Rabbit Risks

The rabbit eating raisins
should be careful
she doesn't turn around
and carry on eating raisins.

(The reason is: the raisins
behind a rabbit aren't raisins.
(A rabbit should be stopping
when it nibbles on a dropping.))

Seen from the Waterloo Train*

Martin has a heron.
A heron has he.
It gives him little honey
since a heron's not a bee.

Martin has a heron.
It eats a lot of fish.
Martin has a heron
and one more wish.

* Martins Heron is one of the odder named railway stations I've seen. I've never got off the train there, so have no idea if it's actually named after a bloke called Martin's favourite pet heron which he mistakenly acquired after rubbing a genie's lamp and accidentally saying what came into his head instead of planning his wishes properly.

Fidget

Bill was a fidget,
she couldn't sit still.

Her mum made her sit
at the top of a hill

with very steep sides
and a lake at the bottom.

The point of all this?
I've clearly forgotten.

Grow Your Own

Where do you go to buy
lamp-post seeds?

I've searched the garden centre
fruitlessly for lamp-post trees.

Perhaps I'll plant a desk lamp
and water it each night.

In time it'll grow taller.
That's how it works, right?

Some Mistakes

The seagull was seasick.
The mountain goat tripped up.
The giraffe looked down.

The wasp sat on its sting.
The snake bit its lip.
The sloth let go.

I wrote this poem.
You read this poem.

Quilt Control

If not watered regularly
your quilt will wilt.

But water it too much
and it might melt.

Proper blanket dampness
is a tricky balancing act,

like juggling a watering can
on top of your brother's bed.

Granny's Glasses

My granny has curtains
on her glasses.

She draws them when she's bored
of what you're saying.

That's your cue to shut up
and consider going home.

After all, it's her house
and she'll be staying.

Bridget

Bridget
no longer goes near rivers
or gorges
or crevasses,

not because
she is allergic
to people saying,
'Bridge it, Bridget',

but because,
she has learnt,
the people who say,
'Bridge it, Bridget',
are allergic to black eyes.

Gravy is not Perfume

People who dab gravy
on their wrists
and below their ears
get eaten by dogs
more often than people who don't.

So if your mother
says to do it,
be sure you say you won't.

Hedgerow Lore

A hedgehog doesn't really hog
 the hedge,
there's room in there for others at
 the edge,
and, of course, up above,
be they sparrow, be they dove,
they'll hang around the hedge until
 they fledge.

35

Busier Than It Looks

Lazy's not
a lazy word.

It goes from one end
of the alphabet
to the other,
no bother,

but don't enquire
too closely
as to its reasons –

it'll give you 'ell
if you ask why.

Bad Song for Good Babies
or
Good Song for Bad Babies

Crabs and vultures,
fleas and stoats.
(Fleas and stoats!)

Crabs and vultures,
fleas and stoats.
(Fleas and stoats!)

And wasps and nettles
and boiling hot kettles.

Crabs and vultures,
fleas and stoats.
(Fleas and stoats!)

Lying Poem

This poem is a fibber.
It tells pork pies.

Don't believe
a single word
that's in it.

All of it is untrue,
especially this bit.

Might as well
just screw it up
and bin it.

Watch Out

Richard
steals sticks
from the dogs
in the park.

Richard
steals stars
from the sky
in the dark.

Richard
steals poos
from the straw
in the hutch,

but nobody's
bothered
by that
very much.

Missing

This poem is missing.
I've looked everywhere.

Under the sofa.
Over here, over there.

I can't seem to find it.
It's missing, it's true.

In this place of that poem ...
will this one do?

Snoring Poem

Look! Here is a poem
lying down on the page.

Tiptoe past, please –
it took me an age

to get it to sleep,
eventually,

and now that it's snoring
let's just let it be.

The Last Doughnut

One last doughnut sitting on the side.
When it sees me coming it tries to hide,
but I'm too fast for it and I open wide
and there's one more doughnut in my
    inside.

Why Children Should Be Strapped Down at All Times

When Zedric is nervous
he jumps in the air

surprising the dentist
who's working right there

on drilling the holes
in the little white teeth

and now in the gums
that are bleeding beneath.

Autumn Hobby

I've saved all the leaves
from the forest floor

and am going back
in the spring
with my glue pot

to do what
I fear,
one year,
nature might forget.

(She hasn't yet.)

And the Wren is the Loudest of Them All

The cat lurks
in the middle of the lawn.

A fat splodge of orange
in green.

From the chirping and clicking
and trilling and crawking

I think that the cat
has been seen.

Quiet

This poem is quiet.
This poem is shy.

This poem will never
look you in the eye.

It murmurs and mutters
and then runs away,

and nobody knows
what it wants to say.

Boring Poem

This poem's a dull one.
It's not made of sparks.

It doesn't have lasers
or rainbows or sharks

or fireworks booming
or cranberry stuffing –

in fact, if you read it,
it's basically nothing.

The Tennis Player's Complaint

'You'd think we still lived in the dark ages.
I mean, yes, I'm a lady, but heavens above!
My racket will cause him an injury soon
if that umpire keeps calling me "Love".'

Book Poem

A book is a knowledge sandwich,
with cardboard bread
and a filling
made of word-flavoured paper.

Don't get carried away with this
    metaphor, though –
librarians start to mutter
when readers start to butter.

Mirror Poem

A mirror
gets clearer
the nearer
you get,

unless it is
covered
with muck
and with wet

gribbly bits
and slimy
with goo.

(Hang on -
I think
the mucky one's
you.)

Me and My Coconuts

I've got a lovely bunch of coconuts.
Ambitious squirrels eye me in the street.
They've never managed to get one off
    me yet.
(Cos I run fast and they've got tiny feet.)

Ecology Poem

Tigers are lovely and stripey and free.
If I met a tiger I'd let it eat me.

I am not lovely or stripey or free.
Better, I say, the tiger than me.

Pancake

Pancakes are good.
Pancakes are great.
Pancake's a food
that I really rate.

Although it's not really much of a cake,
when you think about it,
more a sort of floppy plate.

I Ate All the Cake at the Ballet School

I'm the biggest boy in my ballet class now.
There's them little guys, then there's me.

I strap on my shoes, I do up my hair,
I slip on my frilly threethree.

Not a Lullaby

Rock-a-bye squirrel
in the tree top.
If you bounce a lot
then acorns will drop.

Down you can scamper.
You've done a good job!
Now stuff all the acorns
into your gob.

Packed Lunch Poem

The wolves on the bus go
rarr!, rarr!, rarr!,
rarr!, rarr!, rarr!,
rarr!, rarr!, rarr!,
the wolves on the bus go,
rarr!, rarr!, rarr!,
til all the kids are gone.

Howl!

A Nice Tune

When Sidney the snake
decided to take
piano lessons
they lasted seconds.

Headbutting the keys
didn't please
Mrs Hosannah
who owned the piano.

She slammed the lid
which did for Sid.

Inventing the Humbug

First they tried the hugbug.
It got annoying.

Then they tried the humbum.
It was embarrassing.

Next came the hugbum.
It was embarrassing too.

Finally:
black and white stripes in flight.

Autumn

In the autumn of the year
only two things are clear,
the facts are these:
the leaves leave the trees
except for the evergreens
who leave their leaves in their eaves.

Cobweb Mornings

When the dew is cold
and diamonds glitter
spiders complain
about their tiny cold feet
and their fly-less nets
and how they aren't really thirsty
despite catching all the wets.

Melted Friend

The snow has gone
and the lawn is green.
You can hardly tell
it's even been.

A carrot sits,
an orange shock –
for she who knows
it marks the spot.

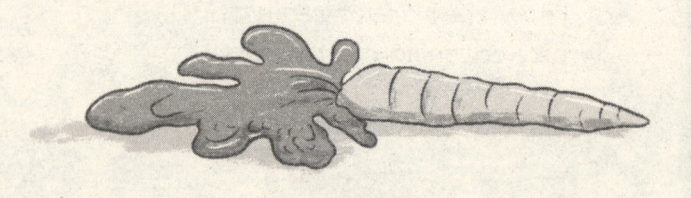

Pumice

The stone in my hand
floats.

Its many-chambered heart
tunnelled with bubbles.

Once the loudest of rocks,
born in deep fire,

now bobs in the bath
and smooths away troubles.

Moon

Coming out of school
and there she is –
a chalk-smudge
finger-dab
of white on blue.

You can see the sky through it
like
your mother's heart
through her frown.

If You Like This Snake Poem, You Shoulda Put a Ring on It

Snakes love doughnuts.

They adore the jam ones most,
think they're the absolute tops.

But they usually buy ring doughnuts
    because,
they're easier to get home from the shops.

Never Trust Your Brother's Advice, Except Maybe Just This Once

I tried to soft-boil my Easter egg,
cos I wanted to dip my soldier,
but it didn't last long in hot water
and my brother said, 'I told ya'.

Spring is Sprung

Watch it fly
excitedly out of your hands,
explosively,
as a sudden bulb goes off,
a yellow trumpet blaring
so loud
so bright
it almost takes your eye out.

Big Summer Poem

It's too hot to pick a pen up.
It's too hot to write a poem.
It's too hot to think about this.
It's too hot. See ya. I'm going.

A Short Poem About Climate Change

A robin redbreast
in a cage
made William Blake
rant and rage.

I dread to think
what Bill would say
if he knew what we do
to them today.

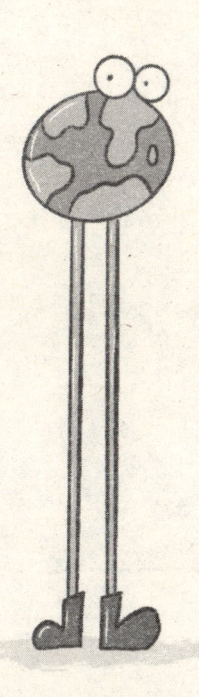

You're Too Low, Get Back Where You Belong

Walking on a foggy day
I only breathe one way –
$\qquad\qquad\qquad$ out.

I don't want clouds
in my lungs,
thank you very much.

I'm not a sky kind of guy.

Pirates

The vegetarian pirate
has a carrot instead of a parrot,
which doesn't make much sense
but is handy if he ever needs
a nutritious snack halfway through the day.

Making an Exhibition of Myself

I went to *The Ideal Mirror Exhibition*
at the London Olympia just last week.

Didn't see any mirrors there.

Lots of pictures of me though.

Seemed a bit odd.

Sometimes

Lines are for going outside of.

Colour's for spilling out.

You be the judge of whether your drawing

is meant to be neat
or is wanting to shout.

Pet Whale Poem

Having a whale for a pet
is not the best bet.

For one thing it'll get
the vet
wet,

and for another
have you tried asking your mother?

The Noonicorn

The noonicorn's horn
shines like daylight –

whatever the time
it's always noon-bright.

Glowing so sunny,
that spike on its head.

(Puts on a horn-cosy
when going to bed.)

On the Protest

NO CUTS
TO
DOUGHNUTS

the woman's placard read.

'Is someone proposing
a doughnut diminution?'
I asked.

'Not that I'm aware of,'
she said.
'I'm just getting in ahead.'

A Quick Thought About Birds

The sky's so grey.
The clouds so low.
The winter's here.
The smart birds go

south to seek
the fleeing sun.
The ones that stay
behind are dumb.

Danger UXB!

Morris munches macaroni.
Charlie chews cheese.
Graham guzzles gravy granules.
Peter asks them, 'Please

stop, I'm trying to defuse this bomb
and you're all being very distracting.'

Beard Poem

Look at the bald man with a beard.
(Don't stare, don't gawp, don't frown.)
If you squint a little as you look:
his head's on upside down.

Burger Tips

Brown and crispy
dripping with juice
I like my burgers
made from moose,
but little bones
can make you cough
so I always saw
the antlers off.

Day Dream Troll

Under the bridge
the little troll hides.

The goats are gruff
and big.

She wishes she were
a brave old wolf

puffing her teeth
at a pig.

The Maths of Snakes

Adders
are subtractors
if they bite hard enough

and
multipliers
if they do the egg dance.

This sort of wordplayful poem is,

I have been told,

divisive.

Pacifist Poem

I want to watch
unboxing videos –

men in the ring
refusing to fight.

I want to think,
despite everything,

maybe this world
will turn out alright.

Railway Sketch

Pigeons
brave as tigers
hunt crumbs
along the platform.

I watch them
stalk specks
as the station
slides away.

They seem
unbothered
by the smooth
move.

Can You Remember a Secret?

Our teacher has bats in her belfry,
she's got skeletons in her closet,
she's got ghosts in her cutlery drawer
and vampires ... oh, where was it?

Three True Facts and a Lie

Milk comes from cows.
Water comes from clouds.

Honey comes from bees.
And wind comes from trees

waving all their arms
and wafting with their leaves.

See What Morning Brings

I left an armadillo
under my pillow.

In the night
to my delight

the Armadillo Fairy popped round,
liked what it found,

and left me
50p.

Playing with Pets

Some kids play fetch with their dogs
and spoil them with all of their love.

Some kids play catch with hedgehogs,
but they only spoil their gloves.

Plankton

Some plankton I know
had difficulty getting to sleep at night.

Went out and bought one of those
 relaxation tapes –
Pacific Whale Song.

Didn't help much.

Fish

Why are fish so happy?
All they do is swim and feed.

But they never wear a nappy
so they swim in what they peed.

Travel Writing

Lumpy landscapes
in the rain

are best explored
in the brain

by picking up
a book or map

then dreaming
as you take a nap.

Jam

What are Jammie Dodgers dodging?

Presumably things that would
 otherwise lodge in
the jam in the middle

or the biscuity bit.

I guess that's it.

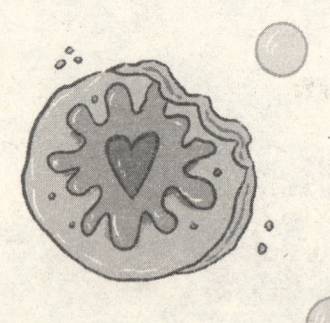

Bubbly Old Lady

We save money in our house
by not buying bubble bath.
We just sit gran in the tub
and try to make her laugh.

A Bath Poem

If there's a fire in the house
don't scream and run and shout.
Just sit tight in the bath
and splash it all about.

The Dangers of Rock and Roll

Don't put a rock in a roll,
unless you hate having teeth.

And be careful when rolling rocks,
in case you end up underneath.

Rhinoceroses Try Their Best

Rhinos have poor eyesight.
To them you're just a blur.

Don't fret if one calls you Mr when you're a Ms (or vice versa).

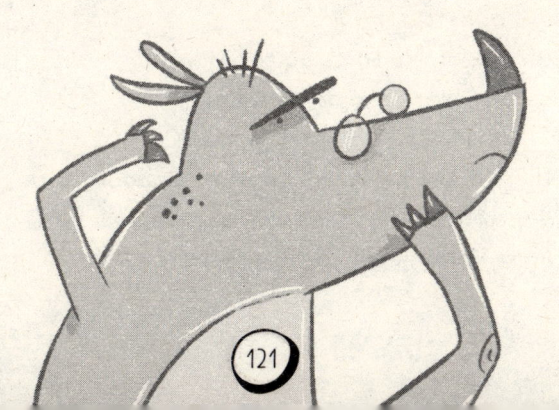

Reasons, Not Necessarily Good Ones

I eat my chips with mushy bees.
I've done it all my life.
It makes them taste quite stingy
and it irritates my wife.*

*Eagle-eyed super knowledgeable poetry brain-boxes will realise this is just a version of the famous poem by Anonymous that goes:

I eat my peas with honey,
I've done it all my life.
It makes them taste quite funny
but it keeps them on the knife.

There are some other poems in this book which are versions of other pre-existing poems by Anonymous. See if you can find them.

Life-Cycles

The nymph dreams
of streams
seen from above.

Fresh-flowing water
that gleams
in the light,
sparkles, flashing-bright,
below
the dragonfly
finally
burst into flight.

How to Save the World (Climate Change Poem)

Be better than your mum and dad.

That's all.

Just promise you'll be not as bad.

Don't fall
into the habits that they had.

Finding the Balance

If mud tasted like chocolate
the countryside would be cleaner,

but the rules against eating out of doors
would probably be much meaner.

The Shy Chef

Nancy hates it
if people crowd her
when she makes her famous
spicy fish chowder.

But not as much
as the fish do.

Bad Mayo Poem

Why'd I hire a witch
to run my sandwich shop?

She puts newt legs in the mayo
and we all wish she'd stop.

23

Yo Ho Ho and a Bottle of Diet Coke Please If You Don't Mind, Thank You Ever So Much (a poem for polite pirates)

Fifteen men on the dead man's chest,
 the dead man's growing flatter.
You'd only fit seven on
 if some of them were fatter.

Wisdom

A sausage a day
keeps the vegetarian away,

unless they're veggie sausages
in which case
you ought
to share
(if you're feeling fair).

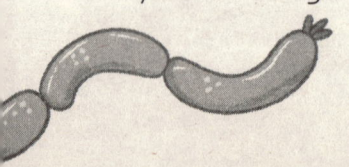

A Lesson on the Art of Storytelling

Even the longest story starts
with a single step,

but if it treads onto a tiger's tail
that's all the story you get.

The Truth About Being a Poet

Sometimes the poem I'm writing
loses confidence
before I finish writing it down.

Nevertheless, I usually keep going
despite the reader's
growing
frown.

Little Spring Poem

The blossom's
so beautiful today,
it's getting hard to tell,
looking from here,
what's a bumbling flower
and what's a breeze-nodding bee.

Hospital Visiting Poem

here! look!
I've brought you
this refreshing
bunch of grape

forgive me
the bus ride was long
and the day was hot

Pet Slug Poem

If your pet slug's
big enough for hugs,

well, I'd ask your dad to bring
the *Guinness Book of Records* people in.

Pet Canary Poem

There's nothing quite as scary
as an overweight canary.

If it weighs more than you do,
you'll be knee-deep in doo-doo.

The Melody

The record on the player spins.
The needle scratches in the groove.
Silent, distant grandma grins.
Her far-back foot begins to move.

Not a Bike Poem

My bike
had bricks
for wheels,

and for a saddle,

and for a frame.

It was a shame.

It was a house.

Bench Poem

It's early morning,
January.

On the train platform
the bench
is ready to bite
tired people's bums
with its diamond
sparkles.

Halloween Blues

Never mind
all my *woo-oo-oo*-ing
 and waving arms,
all my draped sheets
 and rattling chains,
she always saw straight through me.

Spoon Poem

Tiny bowl
on a stick

help me do
this magic trick –

see this custard,
yellow, thick?

Make it disappear,
dead quick.

Sad Song of the Sea

Ethel was the mermaid
no one wanted to kiss.
Her bottom half was human
and her top half made of fish.

Why is Frances So Annoying?

Frances
dances
dances
every night.

Frances
dances
dances
every day.

Frances
dances
dances
of delight.

Frances'
neighbours
wish she'd
go away.

The Rabbit's Prayer

Let us have lettuce today.
Let us have lettuce tomorrow.
Let us have lettuce everyday
and carrots please to follow.

Pet Crocodile Poem

A crocodile's a tricky pet
by the time you get

it to sit on your lap
it's probably gone SNAP!

Body Poem

Everywhere I go
I take this bag of skin –
it's the best thing I've found
to keep my bones in.

Glasses

I went for one of those
free eye-tests at the Optimist's the other day.

He said things were looking up.

The Problem of the Wrong Oblong

My oblong's gone wrong.
(Look, just over there.)
Two sides are too short ...

I'll call it a square.

Problem solved.

January's Gift

January turns up, dumps frost
 and mist
  and walks away,

like a litterbug
giving the world
a fresh cold shoulder.

Wriggly Big Snake Poem

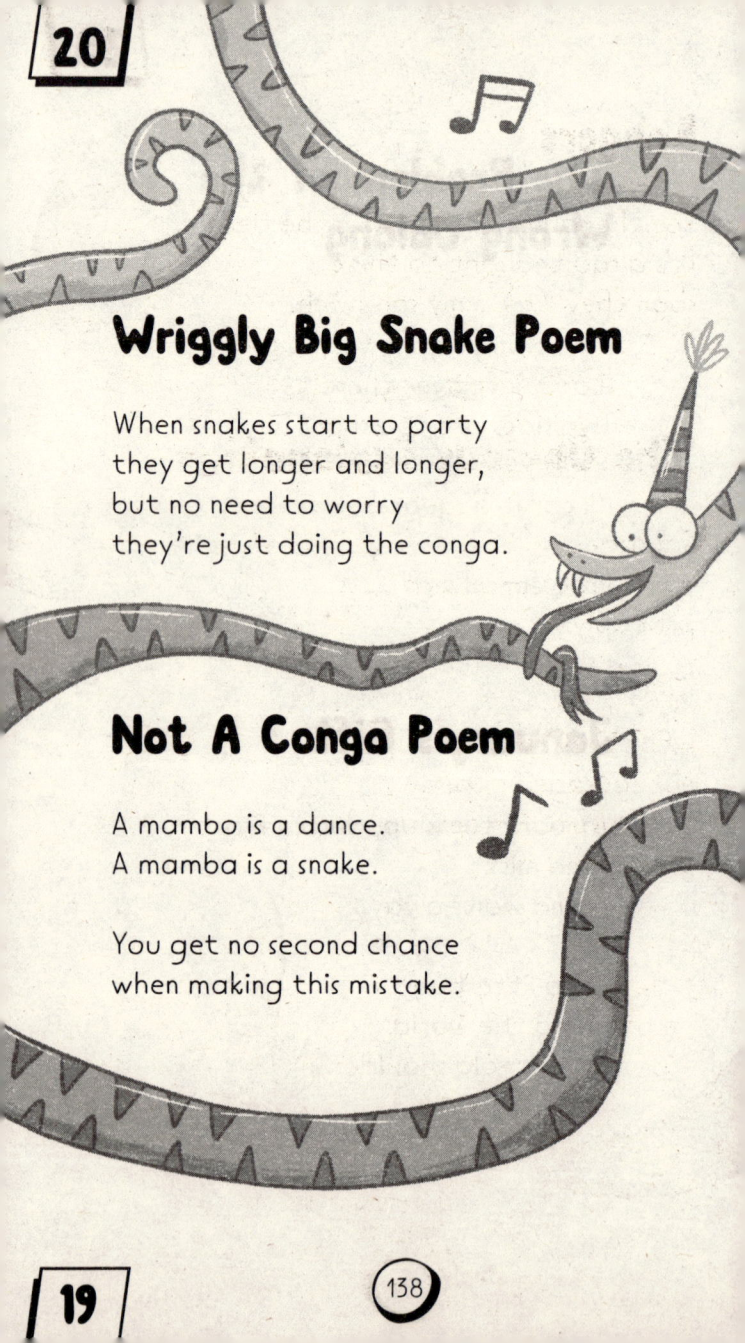

When snakes start to party
they get longer and longer,
but no need to worry
they're just doing the conga.

Not A Conga Poem

A mambo is a dance.
A mamba is a snake.

You get no second chance
when making this mistake.

Bangers

See the sausages running in the field.
It's a sad thought to think
soon they'll be in my sandwich.

The Obvious Explanation

Sausages
come in all shapes and sizes,
probably.

But,
when they're
not sausage-shaped
they just don't get named
properly.

Always Check Your Boots First

A wolf in your wellies
will worry your toes,
with its pointy hard teeth
and its shocking wet nose.

Happy Smiley Squirrels

Take your picnic basket
up a tree.

Spreading the picnic cloth
is awkward,

but the squirrels
appreciate
the company.

Bread Roll Poem

Fluffy in the middle,
crusty round the edge,

a little like the tummy
of a lovely little hedge-

hog.

Horse Poem

Hay in.
Hay out.

Stand in field.
Run about.

Flick tail.
Long nose.

I'm a horse,
I suppose.

At The Circus

Gaston
gives
good glares.

Susan
sends
serious stares.

Phyllis
flashes
fearsome frowns.

These three
aren't
the funniest clowns.

Spring Poem

After winter's chills
the daffodils'
spills
of sunbright
yellow light
brush the dust
out of the world's eyes.

Winter Note

The robin on the feeder
flutters, flaps and fusses,
nabs a seed and vanishes
back into the bushes.

The Author's Xmas Poem

Christmastime is coming.
The sprouts are growing round.
Books are easy gifts to wrap,
or so I've found.

Don't Mention the Mint Sauce

Mary had a little lamb
for her lunch on Sunday.
Roast potatoes, Yorkshire pud,
and leftovers for Monday.*

* Here's another one.

Pet Cheetah Poem

A pet cheetah won't ever be beaten.
If you dare win a race, prepare to be eaten.

The Feathered Serpent

If you nick
a goose's eggs,

they'll hiss and bite
like a snake with legs

(and wings).

Bubbles

Soup soap
won't get you clean,

unless the soup
the soup soap's

made from's
soap soup.

Sport

Footballs
are mostly air.

Football players
move the air

from here
to there.

Oddly,
people care.

Expectations

I expected a surprise
for my birthday.

Imagine my surprise
when I didn't get one.

Tiny Insult Poem

Your brain's
as much use as
Medusa's
mirror.

(I can't say it
any clearer.)

Wanda Wonders

Wanda
is fond of
fish fingers,

but turns
up her nose
at fish toes.

Brown Things

Toffees
are sticky

so you don't
confuse them
with sticks,

which aren't.

A Desert Proverb

Watch out where the camels stand
and don't you eat that yellow sand.

Poem for When There's a Duckling on Your Chair and You Want to Sit Down

Chuck the duckling off your chair
before you place your bottom there.

Not the Best Poem in the World

If my imaginative powers were stronger
this poem would probably be longer.

Poem About a Wasp at a Garden Party Attacking the Person Playing the Guitar

Striped and shining,
porcupining,
I wing along
and sting a song.

Testimony of a Medieval Monk

I'll illustrate a manuscript;
then I'll sweep the floor a bit.

Kitchen Poem

If you can't stand the heat
get in the fridge.

How to Avoid Upsetting a Serpent on its Birthday

If you wake
the snake
first bake
a cake.

Dirty Foot Poem

12 inches long,
with quite a pong.

Autumn Speaks to the Leaves

'Won't you *please* get off the trees?'

Spring Talks to the Trees

'We're not stopping.
Buds – get popping!'

In the Pet Shop Wondering How Often One Might Need to Buy a Special Cake in Addition to Dog Food

This spaniel?
He

has birthdays
annual-

ly.

Healthy Eating Poem

Do not
do that
doughnut.

Poem About the First Person to Grow So Tired of Scalding Their Fingers Every Time They Plucked a Sprout Out of the Boiling Water That They Swore Next Christmas They'd Definitely Do Something About It

Advent calendar?
Invent colander.

Poem Dedicated to my Cat's Tiny Passengers

Please fleas,
flee fleece.

The Rabbit, After Attempting to Feast on a Snowman's Carrot

Nothe frothe.
Tooth loothe.

Apple Appreciation Poem

Cor!

(&
more.)

On Being Asked to Write a Paradoxical One Word Poem

No.

Full Moon Warning

Bewerewolf!

The Best Poem I Forgot to Write Down

Alphabetical list of poems

A

Always Check Your Boots First............ 140
And the Wren is the Loudest of Them All 82
Ants at the Picnic.............................. 43
Apple Appreciation Poem 158
Are You Ready for the Weather? 8
The Asthmatic Racer 4
At the Circus................................... 142
At the Seaside................................... 56
The Author's Xmas Poem.....................144
Autumn 93
Autumn Hobby...................................81
Autumn Speaks to the Leaves 154

B

Bad Mayo Poem............................... 125
Bad Song for Good Babies or Good Song
for Bad Babies....................................75
Bangers 139
A Bath Poem 119
Beard Poem 107
Bench Poem.....................................131
The Best Poem I Forgot to Write Down..161
Big Summer Poem 98
Birdlife 21
Blue Day 6
Body Poem 136
Book Poem....................................... 85

Boring Poem 84
Bread Roll Poem 141
Bridget 72
Brown Things 149
Bubbles 146
Bubbly Old Lady 119
Burger Tips 108
Busier Than It Looks 74

C

A Camel Carpet 30
Can You Remember a Secret? 112
Can't See the Tree 11
Centipede 62
Cobweb Mornings 93

D

The Dangers of Rock and Roll 120
Danger UXB! 107
Dave's Stories 16
Dawn Choruses 13
Day Dream Troll 108
A Desert Proverb 150
Dirty Foot Poem 153
Don't Mention the Mint Sauce 144
Donor Card 5

E

Early Bird, Late Worm 50
Ecology Poem 87
Edible Arrangements 20
Even Worser 52
An Exercise in Taste 15
Expectations 148

F

The Fastest Man in the World Does the
Washing Up 42
The Feathered Serpent 145
February 27
Fidget 67
Fighting the Waves 45
Finding the Balance 124
Fish 116
Full Moon Warning 160

G

Giraffes Sitting Down 46
Glasses 136
Glasshouses 39
Good Dog 35
Granny's Glasses 71
Gravy is not Perfume 73
Grow Your Own 68

H

Halloween Blues.................................. 132
Halloween Poem 47
Happy Smiley Squirrels 140
Healthy Eating Poem 155
Hedgerow Lore 73
Here, There, Everywhere 26
Horse Poem 141
Hospital Visiting Poem 128
How to Avoid Upsetting a Serpent on its Birthday... 153
How to Save the World (Climate Change Poem)... 124

I

I Ate All the Cake at the Ballet School .. 88
I Love All Words, Even the Misfits 41
If Coconuts were Eggs 57
If You Like This Snake Poem, You Shoulda Put a Ring On It 97
In the Pet Shop Wondering How Often One Might Need to Buy a Special Cake in Addition to Dog Food 155
Inventing the Humbug 92

J

Jam 118
January's Gift 137

Juggles 7
Just a Little Bit of Effort and Look What
We Can Do 53

K

Kitchen Poem 152

L

The Last Doughnut 80
A Lesson on the Art of Storytelling 127
Life-Cycles 123
Little Spring Poem 128
Lying Poem 76

M

Making an Exhibition of Myself 101
Manners Maketh 58
The Maths of Snakes 109
Me and My Coconuts 87
The Melody 130
Melted Friend 94
Mirror Poem 86
Missing 78
Moon 96
My Special Mother 25

N

Never Trust Your Brother's Advice, Except Maybe Just This Once 97
The New Farmer Learns 49
A Nice Tune 91
The Noonicorn 104
A Nose Poem 2
Noses Belong On Your Face 31
Not a Bike Poem 131
Not a Conga Poem 138
Not a Lullaby 89
Not the Best Poem in the World 151

O

The Obvious Explanation 139
On Being Asked to Write a Paradoxical One Word Poem 159
On the Protest 105

P

Pacifist Poem 110
Packed Lunch Poem 90
Pancake 88
The Penguin 9
Pet Canary Poem 129
Pet Cheetah Poem 145
Pet Crocodile Poem 135
Pet Envy 36

Pet Picking Basics 54
Pet Slug Poem 129
Pet Whale Poem.............................. 103
Piece of Pie...................................... 63
Pink Sniffles 48
Pirates 101
Plankton 116
Playing with Pets 115
Poem About a Wasp at a Garden Party Attacking the Person Playing the Guitar.... 151
Poem About Riding a Slug to School 14
Poem About the First Person to Grow So Tired of Scalding Their Fingers Every Time They Plucked a Sprout Out of the Boiling Water That They Swore Next Christmas They'd Definitely Do Something About It... 156
Poem Dedicated to My Cat's Tiny Passengers 157
Poem for a Baby with Seven Toes 29
Poem For When There's a Duckling on Your Chair and You Want to Sit Down 150
Poetry's Brutal Truth........................ 64
The Problem of the Wrong Oblong 137
Pumice... 95

Q

Questions, Questions, Questions 10
A Quick Thought About Birds 106
Quiet................................... 83
Quilt Control 70

R

The Rabbit, After Attempting to Feast on a Snowman's Carrot 157
Rabbit Risks 65
The Rabbit's Prayer 135
Railway Sketch............................ 111
Ransom....................................52
Reasons, Not Necessarily Good Ones 122
Remembering Good........................... 61
Remembery 19
Rhinoceroses Try Their Best................121
Roots....................................55

S

Sad Song of the Sea 133
School 18
Seagulls Are Smart 62
See What Morning Brings 114
Seen from the Waterloo Train............. 66
A Shellfish Poem 44
A Short Poem About Climate Change....99
The Shy Chef................................. 125

Silences 24
Sky Poem.................................... 17
Snake Poem 1
Snoring Poem 79
Snow Today, Gone Tomorrow 37
Some Mistakes.............................. 69
Sometimes.................................. 102
Spoon Poem 132
Sport 147
Spots and Dots............................. 33
Spring is Sprung 98
Spring Poem................................ 143
Spring Talks to the Trees 154
Strawberry Poem........................... 34
Summertime (and I'm Glad I'm not a Penguin).................................... 38

T

The Tennis Player's Complaint 85
Testimony of a Medieval Monk 152
This Poem is Not a Red Herring........... 23
Three True Facts and a Lie................113
Tiny Insult Poem 148
To Be a Brick 22
Travel Writing 117
Trees Do Like Squirrels Too................ 3
The Truth About Being a Poet 127

U
Umbrella Poem 32

V
Very Berry 12

W
Wanda Wonders 149
Watch Out 77
What Are Poems Made Of? 28
Why Books are Better than Apples 51
Why Children Should be Strapped Down At All Times 80
Why Dave Shouldn't Be Allowed to Name Things Anymore 59
Why is Frances So Annoying? 134
Winter Note 60
Winter Note 143
Wisdom 126
Wriggly Big Snake Poem 138

Y
Yet More Advice 40
Yo Ho Ho and a Bottle of Diet Coke Please If You Don't Mind, Thank You Ever So Much (a poem for polite pirates) 126
You're Too Low, Get Back Where You Belong 100

Acknowledgements

Some of these poems first appeared occasionally in slightly different forms or with different titles, in the following books, bookmarks and magazines (some then appeared elsewhere as well (I wasn't going to say where, but then I got a bit obsessed and have written it all down (see below!)), because if a poem's any good, why not wave it about in as many places as you can?).

Postcards from the Hedgehog (Two Rivers Press, 2007; illustrated by A.F. Harrold): *Autumn**; *Centipede**; *A Desert Proverb*; *Giraffes Sitting Down**; *Plankton*.
* these ones also appeared in **I Eat Squirrels** (2008)

The Man Who Spent Years in the Bath (Quirkstandard's Alternative, 2008; illustrated by Richard Ponsford): *A Bath Poem**+; *Jam**^; *Kitchen Poem***; *Testimony of a Medieval Monk***.
* these ones also appeared in **I Eat Squirrels** (2008)

** these ones also appeared in **Lies My Mother Never Told Me** (2013)
^ this one also appeared in **Things You Find in a Poet's Beard** (2015)
+ this one also appeared in **The Book of Not Entirely Useful Advice** (2020)

I Eat Squirrels (Quirkstandard's Alternative, 2008; illustrated by A.F. Harrold): *Fish; Glasses; A Nice Tune*; Not the Best Poem in the World*; Pancake; Pirates*; Playing with Pets**; Summertime (and I'm Glad I'm not a Penguin); Yo Ho Ho and a Bottle of Diet Coke Please If You Don't Mind, Thank You Ever So Much (a poem for polite pirates)***.
*these ones also later appeared in **Things You Find in a Poet's Beard** (2015)
** these ones also later appeared in **The Book of Not Entirely Useful Advice** (2020)

Lies My Mother Never Told Me (Burning Eye Books, 2013): *Birdlife**; *Blue Day*; *Fighting the Waves*; *A Shellfish Poem*; *Spring Poem**.
* these ones also later appeared in **Things You Find in a Poet's Beard** (2015)

Limited Edition Poetry Bookmark Series (Nangle Rare Books, 2015): *Spots and Dots*.

Things You Find in a Poet's Beard (Burning Eye Books, 2015; illustrated by Chris Riddell): *The Asthmatic Racer*; *Bangers*; *The Fastest Man in the World Does the Washing Up*; *February*; *Here, There, Everywhere*; *Jam*; *The Tennis Player's Complaint*; *Pet Canary Poem*; *Pet Cheetah Poem*; *School*; *Snow Today, Gone Tomorrow*; *Some Mistakes*; *Spring is Sprung*.

Scoop magazine (2017): *Umbrella Poem**.
* this also later appeared in **The Book of Not Entirely Useful Advice** (2020)

Midnight Feasts (Bloomsbury, 2018; edited by A.F. Harrold (me!) and illustrated by Katy Riddell): *Piece of Pie*.

Poems Out Loud! First Poems to Read and Perform (Penguin, 2019; illustrated by Laurie Stansfield): *Why is Frances So Annoying?*

Spaced Out (Bloomsbury, 2019; anthology edited by James Carter and Brian Moses): *Moon**.
* this also later appeared in *The Book of Not Entirely Useful Advice* (2020)

The Book of Not Entirely Useful Advice (Bloomsbury, 2020; illustrated by Mini Grey): *Burger Tips; The Dangers of Rock and Roll; An Exercise in Taste; Expectations; Gravy is not Perfume; Grow Your Own; Juggles; Missing; The New Farmer Learns; The Problem of the Wrong Oblong; Quiet; Rabbit Risks; Roots; Silences.*

The Best Ever Book of Funny Poems (Macmillan, 2021; anthology edited by Brian Moses): *A Quick Thought About Birds**.
* this also later appeared in **Welcome to Wild Town** (2023)

Poems for 7 Year Olds (Macmillan, 2022; anthology edited by me (still A.F. Harrold!)): *Autumn Speaks to the Leaves**.
* this also appears in the anthology **The Big Amazing Poetry Book**, also from Macmillan, 2022

Welcome to Wild Town (Otter-Barry Books, 2023; with Dom Conlon (we each wrote half the poems in the book, by which I mean we each wrote whole poems by ourselves, not that we each wrote half a poem and then the other poet wrote the other half of the same poem, if you see what I mean), illustrated by Korky Paul): *Early Bird, Late Worm; Packed Lunch Poem; The Rabbit's Prayer; Sometimes.*

This page is blank.

Do not eat it.